Jane Cabrera

PEEK-A-BOO YOU !

little bee books

Peek-a-boo baby,
peek-a-boo. . .

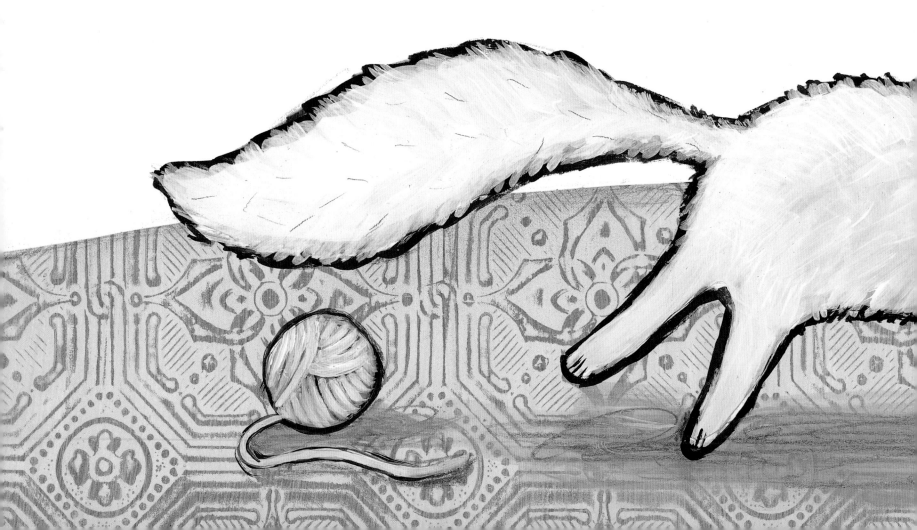

. . . shoe.

Peek-a-boo baby, peek-a-boo . . .

...chew.

Peek-a-boo baby,
peek-a-boo . . .

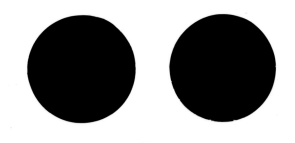

Peek-a-boo baby,
peek-a-boo . . .

...new.

Peek-a-boo baby,
peek-a-boo . . .